The Mission of God

the longest story ever told

Reading order:

01. Intragalaxy First

02. Intragalaxy Final

03. The Sparkling Seashore

04. ACE

05. GEM

06. ZGUYS

07. Mutt Wars

08. Mutt Wars II

09. Pretty One

10. Pretty Two

11. Pretty Three

12. Touch Me

13. Sunn Burnn

14. ... go to Hell

15. Tom

16. Stu

17. Frank

18. Austin

19. Sisters

20. Brothers

21. Baby

22. Pick Me

23. Curfew

24. Gods & Tales

25. Kiss it Bye-Bye, Again!!!

26. All & Truths

27. Tale

28. Tail

29. Tell

30. Tael

31. The Soaring Seahorse

32. Sea Peoples

33. Aliens & Tells

34. Vein

34. Vein

35. Angels & Tails

36. All & All

37. Trolls & Taels

38. Pow-wow with Almighty God...

39. Love Them All

40. Feral Love

41. Arkie

42. Arkie. Barkie.

43. Barkie. Barkie.

44. Uncovered Atlantis

45. The Prez

46. President Trump

47. P.K.

48. Triplet

49. Trip Bet

50. Trip Jet

51. Trip Zet

52. Kiss It, Bye-bye, Baby!!!

53. The Code of God

54. MIA

55 A Tiny Invitation

56. The Hand of God

57. The Mission of God

58. Face Time

59. Hubby Hole

60. Wubby Hole

61. Trigg

62. Music without Sound

63. A Glass Shelf

64. Sniff, the Sweet Honeysuckles

65. Smell, the Sour Deaths

66. Unknown Me

67. Unknown Space

68. Unknown Time

69. Unknown Place

70. Visitards

71. Fire Star

72. Five Stars

73. Four Stars

74. E=mc*q

75. Lost Star

Other Novels

Royal Series

Prince Wars

Princess Wars

King Wars

Aim High

Aim Higher

Aim Highest

Eat My first bullet

Author Notes:

I

have

created

a

personal

and

private

Book

System

for

each

one

of

my

novels

for

the

and

clever

clever

curious

reader.

Rated G for good stuff.

Rated PG for pretty good stuff.

Rated M for mild stuff.

Rated S for really great stuff.

Rated C for cute stuff.

The

storyline

for

this

novel

is

for

really

great

stuff

with

some

relationships

witty

humor

catfights

teenly

dogfights

with

she-ghosts

and

he-ghosts

appearances.

Thanks for entering my imagination!

Chapter One

The Hairbrush That Learned to Sing

Mara had always been a little absent-minded, but she never thought her forgetfulness would lead to magic. One rainy afternoon, she misplaced her favorite hairbrush—the one with the smooth wooden handle and bristles that never tugged too hard. She searched under the bed, behind the dresser, even in the laundry basket, but it was gone.

The next morning, she found it sitting neatly on her vanity, but something was different. A tiny silver button gleamed on its handle, one she swore had never been there before. Curious, she pressed it.

A warm hum filled the air, and the hairbrush spoke in a gentle, melodic voice. "Good morning, Mara. Shall we begin?"

Mara nearly dropped it. "You… talk?"

"I do more than talk," the brush replied. "I sing, I tell stories, and I remember every hairstyle you've ever loved."

Over the next week, the hairbrush became her morning companion. It sang cheerful tunes while detangling her hair, told her bedtime stories when she couldn't sleep, and even whispered gentle affirmations when she felt low. It remembered the braid her grandmother used to make, the bun she wore to her first dance, and the loose waves she loved on summer days.

But one evening, the brush's voice grew softer. "Mara, I was made to help you remember the beauty in your life. Soon, I will fade."

Mara's chest tightened. "Fade? But I need you."

"You don't," it said kindly. "You've learned to sing to yourself, to tell your own stories, to see your own beauty."

The next morning, the silver button was gone. The brush was just wood and bristles again.

Yet when Mara brushed her hair, she found herself humming the brush's songs, smiling at her reflection—not because of the style, but because she finally saw herself the way the brush had.

And in the quiet, she realized the magic had never left at all.

Undo

Redo
Copy
Export
Rewrite
Modify length
Change tone

The Mission of God
The Mission of God
The Mission of God
The Mission of God
The Mission of God
The Mission of God
The Mission of God
The Mission of God
The Mission of God
The Mission of God
The Mission of God
The Mission of God
The Mission of God
The Mission of God
The Mission of God
The Mission of God
The Mission of God
The Mission of God
The Mission of God
The Mission of God
The Mission of God
The Mission of God
The Mission of God
The Mission of God
The Mission of God
The Mission of God
The Mission of God
The Mission of God
The Mission of God
The Mission of God
The Mission of God
The Mission of God
The Mission of God
The Mission of God
The Mission of God
The Mission of God
The Mission of God
The Mission of God
The Mission of God
The Mission of God
The Mission of God

The Mission of God
The Mission of God
The Mission of God
The Mission of God
The Mission of God
The Mission of God
The Mission of God
The Mission of God
The Mission of God
The Mission of God
The Mission of God
The Mission of God
The Mission of God
The Mission of God
The Mission of God
The Mission of God
The Mission of God
The Mission of God
The Mission of God
The Mission of God
The Mission of God
The Mission of God
The Mission of God
The Mission of God
The Mission of God
The Mission of God
The Mission of God
The Mission of God
The Mission of God
The Mission of God
The Mission of God
The Mission of God
The Mission of God
The Mission of God
The Mission of God
The Mission of God
The Mission of God
The Mission of God
The Mission of God
The Mission of God

The Mission of God
The Mission of God
The Mission of God
The Mission of God
The Mission of God
The Mission of God
The Mission of God
The Mission of God
The Mission of God
The Mission of God
The Mission of God
The Mission of God
The Mission of God
The Mission of God
The Mission of God
The Mission of God
The Mission of God
The Mission of God
The Mission of God
The Mission of God
The Mission of God
The Mission of God
The Mission of God
The Mission of God
The Mission of God
The Mission of God
The Mission of God
The Mission of God
The Mission of God
The Mission of God
The Mission of God
The Mission of God
The Mission of God
The Mission of God
The Mission of God
The Mission of God
The Mission of God
The Mission of God
The Mission of God

The Mission of God
The Mission of God
The Mission of God
The Mission of God
The Mission of God
The Mission of God
The Mission of God
The Mission of God
The Mission of God
The Mission of God
The Mission of God
The Mission of God
The Mission of God
The Mission of God
The Mission of God
The Mission of God
The Mission of God
The Mission of God
The Mission of God
The Mission of God
The Mission of God
The Mission of God
The Mission of God
The Mission of God
The Mission of God
The Mission of God
The Mission of God
The Mission of God
The Mission of God
The Mission of God
The Mission of God
The Mission of God
The Mission of God
The Mission of God
The Mission of God
The Mission of God
The Mission of God
The Mission of God
The Mission of God
The Mission of God

The Mission of God
The Mission of God
The Mission of God
The Mission of God
The Mission of God
The Mission of God
The Mission of God
The Mission of God
The Mission of God
The Mission of God
The Mission of God
The Mission of God
The Mission of God
The Mission of God
The Mission of God
The Mission of God
The Mission of God
The Mission of God
The Mission of God
The Mission of God
The Mission of God
The Mission of God
The Mission of God
The Mission of God
The Mission of God
The Mission of God
The Mission of God
The Mission of God
The Mission of God
The Mission of God
The Mission of God
The Mission of God
The Mission of God
The Mission of God
The Mission of God
The Mission of God
The Mission of God
The Mission of God
The Mission of God
The Mission of God

The Mission of God
The Mission of God
The Mission of God
The Mission of God
The Mission of God
The Mission of God
The Mission of God
The Mission of God
The Mission of God
The Mission of God
The Mission of God
The Mission of God
The Mission of God
The Mission of God
The Mission of God
The Mission of God
The Mission of God
The Mission of God
The Mission of God
The Mission of God
The Mission of God
The Mission of God
The Mission of God
The Mission of God
The Mission of God
The Mission of God
The Mission of God
The Mission of God
The Mission of God
The Mission of God
The Mission of God
The Mission of God
The Mission of God
The Mission of God
The Mission of God
The Mission of God
The Mission of God
The Mission of God
The Mission of God
The Mission of God
The Mission of God
The Mission of God

The Mission of God
The Mission of God
The Mission of God
The Mission of God
The Mission of God
The Mission of God
The Mission of God
The Mission of God
The Mission of God
The Mission of God
The Mission of God
The Mission of God
The Mission of God
The Mission of God
The Mission of God
The Mission of God
The Mission of God
The Mission of God
The Mission of God
The Mission of God
The Mission of God
The Mission of God
The Mission of God
The Mission of God
The Mission of God
The Mission of God
The Mission of God
The Mission of God
The Mission of God
The Mission of God
The Mission of God
The Mission of God
The Mission of God
The Mission of God
The Mission of God
The Mission of God
The Mission of God
The Mission of God
The Mission of God
The Mission of God
The Mission of God
The Mission of God

The Mission of God
The Mission of God
The Mission of God
The Mission of God
The Mission of God
The Mission of God
The Mission of God
The Mission of God
The Mission of God
The Mission of God
The Mission of God
The Mission of God
The Mission of God
The Mission of God
The Mission of God
The Mission of God
The Mission of God
The Mission of God
The Mission of God
The Mission of God
The Mission of God
The Mission of God
The Mission of God
The Mission of God
The Mission of God
The Mission of God
The Mission of God
The Mission of God
The Mission of God
The Mission of God
The Mission of God
The Mission of God
The Mission of God
The Mission of God
The Mission of God
The Mission of God
The Mission of God
The Mission of God
The Mission of God

The Mission of God
The Mission of God
The Mission of God
The Mission of God
The Mission of God
The Mission of God
The Mission of God
The Mission of God
The Mission of God
The Mission of God
The Mission of God
The Mission of God
The Mission of God
The Mission of God
The Mission of God
The Mission of God
The Mission of God
The Mission of God
The Mission of God
The Mission of God
The Mission of God
The Mission of God
The Mission of God
The Mission of God
The Mission of God
The Mission of God
The Mission of God
The Mission of God
The Mission of God
The Mission of God
The Mission of God
The Mission of God
The Mission of God
The Mission of God
The Mission of God
The Mission of God
The Mission of God

The Mission of God
The Mission of God
The Mission of God
The Mission of God
The Mission of God
The Mission of God
The Mission of God
The Mission of God
The Mission of God
The Mission of God
The Mission of God
The Mission of God
The Mission of God
The Mission of God
The Mission of God
The Mission of God
The Mission of God
The Mission of God
The Mission of God
The Mission of God
The Mission of God
The Mission of God
The Mission of God
The Mission of God
The Mission of God
The Mission of God
The Mission of God
The Mission of God
The Mission of God
The Mission of God
The Mission of God
The Mission of God
The Mission of God
The Mission of God
The Mission of God
The Mission of God
The Mission of God
The Mission of God
The Mission of God
The Mission of God
The Mission of God

The Mission of God
The Mission of God
The Mission of God
The Mission of God
The Mission of God
The Mission of God
The Mission of God
The Mission of God
The Mission of God
The Mission of God
The Mission of God
The Mission of God
The Mission of God
The Mission of God
The Mission of God
The Mission of God
The Mission of God
The Mission of God
The Mission of God
The Mission of God
The Mission of God
The Mission of God
The Mission of God
The Mission of God
The Mission of God
The Mission of God
The Mission of God
The Mission of God
The Mission of God
The Mission of God
The Mission of God
The Mission of God
The Mission of God
The Mission of God
The Mission of God
The Mission of God
The Mission of God
The Mission of God

The Mission of God
The Mission of God
The Mission of God
The Mission of God
The Mission of God
The Mission of God
The Mission of God
The Mission of God
The Mission of God
The Mission of God
The Mission of God
The Mission of God
The Mission of God
The Mission of God
The Mission of God
The Mission of God
The Mission of God
The Mission of God
The Mission of God
The Mission of God
The Mission of God
The Mission of God
The Mission of God
The Mission of God
The Mission of God
The Mission of God
The Mission of God
The Mission of God
The Mission of God
The Mission of God
The Mission of God
The Mission of God
The Mission of God
The Mission of God
The Mission of God
The Mission of God
The Mission of God
The Mission of God
The Mission of God
The Mission of God
The Mission of God
The Mission of God

The Mission of God
The Mission of God
The Mission of God
The Mission of God
The Mission of God
The Mission of God
The Mission of God
The Mission of God
The Mission of God
The Mission of God
The Mission of God
The Mission of God
The Mission of God
The Mission of God
The Mission of God
The Mission of God
The Mission of God
The Mission of God
The Mission of God
The Mission of God
The Mission of God
The Mission of God
The Mission of God
The Mission of God
The Mission of God
The Mission of God
The Mission of God
The Mission of God
The Mission of God
The Mission of God
The Mission of God
The Mission of God
The Mission of God
The Mission of God
The Mission of God
The Mission of God
The Mission of God
The Mission of God
The Mission of God
The Mission of God
The Mission of God
The Mission of God
The Mission of God
The Mission of God

The Mission of God
The Mission of God
The Mission of God
The Mission of God
The Mission of God
The Mission of God
The Mission of God
The Mission of God
The Mission of God
The Mission of God
The Mission of God
The Mission of God
The Mission of God
The Mission of God
The Mission of God
The Mission of God
The Mission of God
The Mission of God
The Mission of God
The Mission of God
The Mission of God
The Mission of God
The Mission of God
The Mission of God
The Mission of God
The Mission of God
The Mission of God
The Mission of God
The Mission of God
The Mission of God
The Mission of God
The Mission of God
The Mission of God
The Mission of God
The Mission of God
The Mission of God
The Mission of God
The Mission of God
The Mission of God
The Mission of God

The Mission of God
The Mission of God
The Mission of God
The Mission of God
The Mission of God
The Mission of God
The Mission of God
The Mission of God
The Mission of God
The Mission of God
The Mission of God
The Mission of God
The Mission of God
The Mission of God
The Mission of God
The Mission of God
The Mission of God
The Mission of God
The Mission of God
The Mission of God
The Mission of God
The Mission of God
The Mission of God
The Mission of God
The Mission of God
The Mission of God
The Mission of God
The Mission of God
The Mission of God
The Mission of God
The Mission of God
The Mission of God
The Mission of God
The Mission of God
The Mission of God
The Mission of God
The Mission of God
The Mission of God

The Mission of God
The Mission of God
The Mission of God
The Mission of God
The Mission of God
The Mission of God
The Mission of God
The Mission of God
The Mission of God
The Mission of God
The Mission of God
The Mission of God
The Mission of God
The Mission of God
The Mission of God
The Mission of God
The Mission of God
The Mission of God
The Mission of God
The Mission of God
The Mission of God
The Mission of God
The Mission of God
The Mission of God
The Mission of God
The Mission of God
The Mission of God
The Mission of God
The Mission of God
The Mission of God
The Mission of God
The Mission of God
The Mission of God
The Mission of God
The Mission of God
The Mission of God
The Mission of God
The Mission of God
The Mission of God
The Mission of God
The Mission of God

The Mission of God
The Mission of God
The Mission of God
The Mission of God
The Mission of God
The Mission of God
The Mission of God
The Mission of God
The Mission of God
The Mission of God
The Mission of God
The Mission of God
The Mission of God
The Mission of God
The Mission of God
The Mission of God
The Mission of God
The Mission of God
The Mission of God
The Mission of God
The Mission of God
The Mission of God
The Mission of God
The Mission of God
The Mission of God
The Mission of God
The Mission of God
The Mission of God
The Mission of God
The Mission of God
The Mission of God
The Mission of God
The Mission of God
The Mission of God
The Mission of God
The Mission of God
The Mission of God
The Mission of God
The Mission of God

The Mission of God
The Mission of God
The Mission of God
The Mission of God
The Mission of God
The Mission of God
The Mission of God
The Mission of God
The Mission of God
The Mission of God
The Mission of God
The Mission of God
The Mission of God
The Mission of God
The Mission of God
The Mission of God
The Mission of God
The Mission of God
The Mission of God
The Mission of God
The Mission of God
The Mission of God
The Mission of God
The Mission of God
The Mission of God
The Mission of God
The Mission of God
The Mission of God
The Mission of God
The Mission of God
The Mission of God
The Mission of God
The Mission of God
The Mission of God
The Mission of God
The Mission of God
The Mission of God
The Mission of God

The Mission of God
The Mission of God
The Mission of God
The Mission of God
The Mission of God
The Mission of God
The Mission of God
The Mission of God
The Mission of God
The Mission of God
The Mission of God
The Mission of God
The Mission of God
The Mission of God
The Mission of God
The Mission of God
The Mission of God
The Mission of God
The Mission of God
The Mission of God
The Mission of God
The Mission of God
The Mission of God
The Mission of God
The Mission of God
The Mission of God
The Mission of God
The Mission of God
The Mission of God
The Mission of God
The Mission of God
The Mission of God
The Mission of God
The Mission of God
The Mission of God
The Mission of God
The Mission of God
The Mission of God
The Mission of God
The Mission of God
The Mission of God

The Mission of God
The Mission of God
The Mission of God
The Mission of God
The Mission of God
The Mission of God
The Mission of God
The Mission of God
The Mission of God
The Mission of God
The Mission of God
The Mission of God
The Mission of God
The Mission of God
The Mission of God
The Mission of God
The Mission of God
The Mission of God
The Mission of God
The Mission of God
The Mission of God
The Mission of God
The Mission of God
The Mission of God
The Mission of God
The Mission of God
The Mission of God
The Mission of God
The Mission of God
The Mission of God
The Mission of God
The Mission of God
The Mission of God
The Mission of God
The Mission of God
The Mission of God
The Mission of God
The Mission of God
The Mission of God
The Mission of God

The Mission of God
The Mission of God
The Mission of God
The Mission of God
The Mission of God
The Mission of God
The Mission of God
The Mission of God
The Mission of God
The Mission of God
The Mission of God
The Mission of God
The Mission of God
The Mission of God
The Mission of God
The Mission of God
The Mission of God
The Mission of God
The Mission of God
The Mission of God
The Mission of God
The Mission of God
The Mission of God
The Mission of God
The Mission of God
The Mission of God
The Mission of God
The Mission of God
The Mission of God
The Mission of God
The Mission of God
The Mission of God
The Mission of God
The Mission of God
The Mission of God
The Mission of God
The Mission of God
The Mission of God
The Mission of God
The Mission of God

The Mission of God
The Mission of God
The Mission of God
The Mission of God
The Mission of God
The Mission of God
The Mission of God
The Mission of God
The Mission of God
The Mission of God
The Mission of God
The Mission of God
The Mission of God
The Mission of God
The Mission of God
The Mission of God
The Mission of God
The Mission of God
The Mission of God
The Mission of God
The Mission of God
The Mission of God
The Mission of God
The Mission of God
The Mission of God
The Mission of God
The Mission of God
The Mission of God
The Mission of God
The Mission of God
The Mission of God
The Mission of God
The Mission of God
The Mission of God
The Mission of God
The Mission of God

The Mission of God
The Mission of God
The Mission of God
The Mission of God
The Mission of God
The Mission of God
The Mission of God
The Mission of God
The Mission of God
The Mission of God
The Mission of God
The Mission of God
The Mission of God
The Mission of God
The Mission of God
The Mission of God
The Mission of God
The Mission of God
The Mission of God
The Mission of God
The Mission of God
The Mission of God
The Mission of God
The Mission of God
The Mission of God
The Mission of God
The Mission of God
The Mission of God
The Mission of God
The Mission of God
The Mission of God
The Mission of God
The Mission of God
The Mission of God
The Mission of God
The Mission of God
The Mission of God
The Mission of God
The Mission of God
The Mission of God
The Mission of God
The Mission of God

The Mission of God
The Mission of God
The Mission of God
The Mission of God
The Mission of God
The Mission of God
The Mission of God
The Mission of God
The Mission of God
The Mission of God
The Mission of God
The Mission of God
The Mission of God
The Mission of God
The Mission of God
The Mission of God
The Mission of God
The Mission of God
The Mission of God
The Mission of God
The Mission of God
The Mission of God
The Mission of God
The Mission of God
The Mission of God
The Mission of God
The Mission of God
The Mission of God
The Mission of God
The Mission of God
The Mission of God
The Mission of God
The Mission of God
The Mission of God
The Mission of God
The Mission of God
The Mission of God
The Mission of God
The Mission of God

The Mission of God
The Mission of God
The Mission of God
The Mission of God
The Mission of God
The Mission of God
The Mission of God
The Mission of God
The Mission of God
The Mission of God
The Mission of God
The Mission of God
The Mission of God
The Mission of God
The Mission of God
The Mission of God
The Mission of God
The Mission of God
The Mission of God
The Mission of God
The Mission of God
The Mission of God
The Mission of God
The Mission of God
The Mission of God
The Mission of God
The Mission of God
The Mission of God
The Mission of God
The Mission of God
The Mission of God
The Mission of God
The Mission of God
The Mission of God
The Mission of God
The Mission of God
The Mission of God
The Mission of God
The Mission of God
The Mission of God

The Mission of God
The Mission of God
The Mission of God
The Mission of God
The Mission of God
The Mission of God
The Mission of God
The Mission of God
The Mission of God
The Mission of God
The Mission of God
The Mission of God
The Mission of God
The Mission of God
The Mission of God
The Mission of God
The Mission of God
The Mission of God
The Mission of God
The Mission of God
The Mission of God
The Mission of God
The Mission of God
The Mission of God
The Mission of God
The Mission of God
The Mission of God
The Mission of God
The Mission of God
The Mission of God
The Mission of God
The Mission of God
The Mission of God
The Mission of God
The Mission of God
The Mission of God
The Mission of God
The Mission of God

The Mission of God
The Mission of God
The Mission of God
The Mission of God
The Mission of God
The Mission of God
The Mission of God
The Mission of God
The Mission of God
The Mission of God
The Mission of God
The Mission of God
The Mission of God
The Mission of God
The Mission of God
The Mission of God
The Mission of God
The Mission of God
The Mission of God
The Mission of God
The Mission of God
The Mission of God
The Mission of God
The Mission of God
The Mission of God
The Mission of God
The Mission of God
The Mission of God
The Mission of God
The Mission of God
The Mission of God
The Mission of God
The Mission of God
The Mission of God
The Mission of God
The Mission of God

The Mission of God
The Mission of God
The Mission of God
The Mission of God
The Mission of God
The Mission of God
The Mission of God
The Mission of God
The Mission of God
The Mission of God
The Mission of God
The Mission of God
The Mission of God
The Mission of God
The Mission of God
The Mission of God
The Mission of God
The Mission of God
The Mission of God
The Mission of God
The Mission of God
The Mission of God
The Mission of God
The Mission of God
The Mission of God
The Mission of God
The Mission of God
The Mission of God
The Mission of God
The Mission of God
The Mission of God
The Mission of God
The Mission of God
The Mission of God
The Mission of God
The Mission of God
The Mission of God
The Mission of God
The Mission of God
The Mission of God
The Mission of God
The Mission of God
The Mission of God

The Mission of God
The Mission of God
The Mission of God
The Mission of God
The Mission of God
The Mission of God
The Mission of God
The Mission of God
The Mission of God
The Mission of God
The Mission of God
The Mission of God
The Mission of God
The Mission of God
The Mission of God
The Mission of God
The Mission of God
The Mission of God
The Mission of God
The Mission of God
The Mission of God
The Mission of God
The Mission of God
The Mission of God
The Mission of God
The Mission of God
The Mission of God
The Mission of God
The Mission of God
The Mission of God
The Mission of God
The Mission of God
The Mission of God
The Mission of God
The Mission of God
The Mission of God
The Mission of God

The Mission of God
The Mission of God
The Mission of God
The Mission of God
The Mission of God
The Mission of God
The Mission of God
The Mission of God
The Mission of God
The Mission of God
The Mission of God
The Mission of God
The Mission of God
The Mission of God
The Mission of God
The Mission of God
The Mission of God
The Mission of God
The Mission of God
The Mission of God
The Mission of God
The Mission of God
The Mission of God
The Mission of God
The Mission of God
The Mission of God
The Mission of God
The Mission of God
The Mission of God
The Mission of God
The Mission of God
The Mission of God
The Mission of God
The Mission of God
The Mission of God
The Mission of God
The Mission of God
The Mission of God
The Mission of God
The Mission of God
The Mission of God

The Mission of God
The Mission of God
The Mission of God
The Mission of God
The Mission of God
The Mission of God
The Mission of God
The Mission of God
The Mission of God
The Mission of God
The Mission of God
The Mission of God
The Mission of God
The Mission of God
The Mission of God
The Mission of God
The Mission of God
The Mission of God
The Mission of God
The Mission of God
The Mission of God
The Mission of God
The Mission of God
The Mission of God
The Mission of God
The Mission of God
The Mission of God
The Mission of God
The Mission of God
The Mission of God
The Mission of God
The Mission of God
The Mission of God
The Mission of God
The Mission of God
The Mission of God
The Mission of God
The Mission of God

The Mission of God
The Mission of God
The Mission of God
The Mission of God
The Mission of God
The Mission of God
The Mission of God
The Mission of God
The Mission of God
The Mission of God
The Mission of God
The Mission of God
The Mission of God
The Mission of God
The Mission of God
The Mission of God
The Mission of God
The Mission of God
The Mission of God
The Mission of God
The Mission of God
The Mission of God
The Mission of God
The Mission of God
The Mission of God
The Mission of God
The Mission of God
The Mission of God
The Mission of God
The Mission of God
The Mission of God
The Mission of God
The Mission of God
The Mission of God
The Mission of God
The Mission of God
The Mission of God
The Mission of God

The Mission of God
The Mission of God
The Mission of God
The Mission of God
The Mission of God
The Mission of God
The Mission of God
The Mission of God
The Mission of God
The Mission of God
The Mission of God
The Mission of God
The Mission of God
The Mission of God
The Mission of God
The Mission of God
The Mission of God
The Mission of God
The Mission of God
The Mission of God
The Mission of God
The Mission of God
The Mission of God
The Mission of God
The Mission of God
The Mission of God
The Mission of God
The Mission of God
The Mission of God
The Mission of God
The Mission of God
The Mission of God
The Mission of God
The Mission of God
The Mission of God
The Mission of God
The Mission of God
The Mission of God
The Mission of God
The Mission of God

The Mission of God
The Mission of God
The Mission of God
The Mission of God
The Mission of God
The Mission of God
The Mission of God
The Mission of God
The Mission of God
The Mission of God
The Mission of God
The Mission of God
The Mission of God
The Mission of God
The Mission of God
The Mission of God
The Mission of God
The Mission of God
The Mission of God
The Mission of God
The Mission of God
The Mission of God
The Mission of God
The Mission of God
The Mission of God
The Mission of God
The Mission of God
The Mission of God
The Mission of God
The Mission of God
The Mission of God
The Mission of God
The Mission of God
The Mission of God
The Mission of God
The Mission of God
The Mission of God
The Mission of God
The Mission of God

The Mission of God
The Mission of God
The Mission of God
The Mission of God
The Mission of God
The Mission of God
The Mission of God
The Mission of God
The Mission of God
The Mission of God
The Mission of God
The Mission of God
The Mission of God
The Mission of God
The Mission of God
The Mission of God
The Mission of God
The Mission of God
The Mission of God
The Mission of God
The Mission of God
The Mission of God
The Mission of God
The Mission of God
The Mission of God
The Mission of God
The Mission of God
The Mission of God
The Mission of God
The Mission of God
The Mission of God
The Mission of God
The Mission of God
The Mission of God
The Mission of God
The Mission of God
The Mission of God
The Mission of God
The Mission of God

The Mission of God
The Mission of God
The Mission of God
The Mission of God
The Mission of God
The Mission of God
The Mission of God
The Mission of God
The Mission of God
The Mission of God
The Mission of God
The Mission of God
The Mission of God
The Mission of God
The Mission of God
The Mission of God
The Mission of God
The Mission of God
The Mission of God
The Mission of God
The Mission of God
The Mission of God
The Mission of God
The Mission of God
The Mission of God
The Mission of God
The Mission of God
The Mission of God
The Mission of God
The Mission of God
The Mission of God
The Mission of God
The Mission of God
The Mission of God
The Mission of God
The Mission of God
The Mission of God
The Mission of God
The Mission of God
The Mission of God
The Mission of God

The Mission of God
The Mission of God
The Mission of God
The Mission of God
The Mission of God
The Mission of God
The Mission of God
The Mission of God
The Mission of God
The Mission of God
The Mission of God
The Mission of God
The Mission of God
The Mission of God
The Mission of God
The Mission of God
The Mission of God
The Mission of God
The Mission of God
The Mission of God
The Mission of God
The Mission of God
The Mission of God
The Mission of God
The Mission of God
The Mission of God
The Mission of God
The Mission of God
The Mission of God
The Mission of God
The Mission of God
The Mission of God
The Mission of God
The Mission of God
The Mission of God
The Mission of God
The Mission of God
The Mission of God
The Mission of God
The Mission of God
The Mission of God

The Mission of God
The Mission of God
The Mission of God
The Mission of God
The Mission of God
The Mission of God
The Mission of God
The Mission of God
The Mission of God
The Mission of God
The Mission of God
The Mission of God
The Mission of God
The Mission of God
The Mission of God
The Mission of God
The Mission of God
The Mission of God
The Mission of God
The Mission of God
The Mission of God
The Mission of God
The Mission of God
The Mission of God
The Mission of God
The Mission of God
The Mission of God
The Mission of God
The Mission of God
The Mission of God
The Mission of God
The Mission of God
The Mission of God
The Mission of God
The Mission of God
The Mission of God
The Mission of God
The Mission of God
The Mission of God
The Mission of God
The Mission of God

The Mission of God
The Mission of God
The Mission of God
The Mission of God
The Mission of God
The Mission of God
The Mission of God
The Mission of God
The Mission of God
The Mission of God
The Mission of God
The Mission of God
The Mission of God
The Mission of God
The Mission of God
The Mission of God
The Mission of God
The Mission of God
The Mission of God
The Mission of God
The Mission of God
The Mission of God
The Mission of God
The Mission of God
The Mission of God
The Mission of God
The Mission of God
The Mission of God
The Mission of God
The Mission of God
The Mission of God
The Mission of God
The Mission of God
The Mission of God
The Mission of God
The Mission of God
The Mission of God

The Mission of God
The Mission of God
The Mission of God
The Mission of God
The Mission of God
The Mission of God
The Mission of God
The Mission of God
The Mission of God
The Mission of God
The Mission of God
The Mission of God
The Mission of God
The Mission of God
The Mission of God
The Mission of God
The Mission of God
The Mission of God
The Mission of God
The Mission of God
The Mission of God
The Mission of God
The Mission of God
The Mission of God
The Mission of God
The Mission of God
The Mission of God
The Mission of God
The Mission of God
The Mission of God
The Mission of God
The Mission of God
The Mission of God
The Mission of God
The Mission of God
The Mission of God
The Mission of God
The Mission of God
The Mission of God
The Mission of God

The Mission of God
The Mission of God
The Mission of God
The Mission of God
The Mission of God
The Mission of God
The Mission of God
The Mission of God
The Mission of God
The Mission of God
The Mission of God
The Mission of God
The Mission of God
The Mission of God
The Mission of God
The Mission of God
The Mission of God
The Mission of God
The Mission of God
The Mission of God
The Mission of God
The Mission of God
The Mission of God
The Mission of God
The Mission of God
The Mission of God
The Mission of God
The Mission of God
The Mission of God
The Mission of God
The Mission of God
The Mission of God
The Mission of God
The Mission of God
The Mission of God
The Mission of God
The Mission of God

The Mission of God
The Mission of God
The Mission of God
The Mission of God
The Mission of God
The Mission of God
The Mission of God
The Mission of God
The Mission of God
The Mission of God
The Mission of God
The Mission of God
The Mission of God
The Mission of God
The Mission of God
The Mission of God
The Mission of God
The Mission of God
The Mission of God
The Mission of God
The Mission of God
The Mission of God
The Mission of God
The Mission of God
The Mission of God
The Mission of God
The Mission of God
The Mission of God
The Mission of God
The Mission of God
The Mission of God
The Mission of God
The Mission of God
The Mission of God
The Mission of God
The Mission of God
The Mission of God
The Mission of God
The Mission of God
The Mission of God
The Mission of God
The Mission of God

The Mission of God
The Mission of God
The Mission of God
The Mission of God
The Mission of God
The Mission of God
The Mission of God
The Mission of God
The Mission of God
The Mission of God
The Mission of God
The Mission of God
The Mission of God
The Mission of God
The Mission of God
The Mission of God
The Mission of God
The Mission of God
The Mission of God
The Mission of God
The Mission of God
The Mission of God
The Mission of God
The Mission of God
The Mission of God
The Mission of God
The Mission of God
The Mission of God
The Mission of God
The Mission of God
The Mission of God
The Mission of God
The Mission of God
The Mission of God
The Mission of God
The Mission of God
The Mission of God
The Mission of God
The Mission of God

The Mission of God
The Mission of God
The Mission of God
The Mission of God
The Mission of God
The Mission of God
The Mission of God
The Mission of God
The Mission of God
The Mission of God
The Mission of God
The Mission of God
The Mission of God
The Mission of God
The Mission of God
The Mission of God
The Mission of God
The Mission of God
The Mission of God
The Mission of God
The Mission of God
The Mission of God
The Mission of God
The Mission of God
The Mission of God
The Mission of God
The Mission of God
The Mission of God
The Mission of God
The Mission of God
The Mission of God
The Mission of God
The Mission of God
The Mission of God
The Mission of God
The Mission of God
The Mission of God
The Mission of God
The Mission of God

The Mission of God
The Mission of God
The Mission of God
The Mission of God
The Mission of God
The Mission of God
The Mission of God
The Mission of God
The Mission of God
The Mission of God
The Mission of God
The Mission of God
The Mission of God
The Mission of God
The Mission of God
The Mission of God
The Mission of God
The Mission of God
The Mission of God
The Mission of God
The Mission of God
The Mission of God
The Mission of God
The Mission of God
The Mission of God
The Mission of God
The Mission of God
The Mission of God
The Mission of God
The Mission of God
The Mission of God
The Mission of God
The Mission of God
The Mission of God
The Mission of God
The Mission of God

The Mission of God
The Mission of God
The Mission of God
The Mission of God
The Mission of God
The Mission of God
The Mission of God
The Mission of God
The Mission of God
The Mission of God
The Mission of God
The Mission of God
The Mission of God
The Mission of God
The Mission of God
The Mission of God
The Mission of God
The Mission of God
The Mission of God
The Mission of God
The Mission of God
The Mission of God
The Mission of God
The Mission of God
The Mission of God
The Mission of God
The Mission of God
The Mission of God
The Mission of God
The Mission of God
The Mission of God
The Mission of God
The Mission of God
The Mission of God
The Mission of God
The Mission of God
The Mission of God
The Mission of God
The Mission of God
The Mission of God
The Mission of God
The Mission of God
The Mission of God
The Mission of God

The Mission of God
The Mission of God
The Mission of God
The Mission of God
The Mission of God
The Mission of God
The Mission of God
The Mission of God
The Mission of God
The Mission of God
The Mission of God
The Mission of God
The Mission of God
The Mission of God
The Mission of God
The Mission of God
The Mission of God
The Mission of God
The Mission of God
The Mission of God
The Mission of God
The Mission of God
The Mission of God
The Mission of God
The Mission of God
The Mission of God
The Mission of God
The Mission of God
The Mission of God
The Mission of God
The Mission of God
The Mission of God
The Mission of God
The Mission of God
The Mission of God
The Mission of God
The Mission of God

The Mission of God
The Mission of God
The Mission of God
The Mission of God
The Mission of God
The Mission of God
The Mission of God
The Mission of God
The Mission of God
The Mission of God
The Mission of God
The Mission of God
The Mission of God
The Mission of God
The Mission of God
The Mission of God
The Mission of God
The Mission of God
The Mission of God
The Mission of God
The Mission of God
The Mission of God
The Mission of God
The Mission of God
The Mission of God
The Mission of God
The Mission of God
The Mission of God
The Mission of God
The Mission of God
The Mission of God
The Mission of God
The Mission of God
The Mission of God
The Mission of God
The Mission of God
The Mission of God
The Mission of God
The Mission of God
The Mission of God
The Mission of God
The Mission of God

The Mission of God
The Mission of God
The Mission of God
The Mission of God
The Mission of God
The Mission of God
The Mission of God
The Mission of God
The Mission of God
The Mission of God
The Mission of God
The Mission of God
The Mission of God
The Mission of God
The Mission of God
The Mission of God
The Mission of God
The Mission of God
The Mission of God
The Mission of God
The Mission of God
The Mission of God
The Mission of God
The Mission of God
The Mission of God
The Mission of God
The Mission of God
The Mission of God
The Mission of God
The Mission of God
The Mission of God
The Mission of God
The Mission of God
The Mission of God
The Mission of God
The Mission of God
The Mission of God
The Mission of God
The Mission of God

The Mission of God
The Mission of God
The Mission of God
The Mission of God
The Mission of God
The Mission of God
The Mission of God
The Mission of God
The Mission of God
The Mission of God
The Mission of God
The Mission of God
The Mission of God
The Mission of God
The Mission of God
The Mission of God
The Mission of God
The Mission of God
The Mission of God
The Mission of God
The Mission of God
The Mission of God
The Mission of God
The Mission of God
The Mission of God
The Mission of God
The Mission of God
The Mission of God
The Mission of God
The Mission of God
The Mission of God
The Mission of God
The Mission of God
The Mission of God
The Mission of God
The Mission of God
The Mission of God
The Mission of God
The Mission of God

The Mission of God
The Mission of God
The Mission of God
The Mission of God
The Mission of God
The Mission of God
The Mission of God
The Mission of God
The Mission of God
The Mission of God
The Mission of God
The Mission of God
The Mission of God
The Mission of God
The Mission of God
The Mission of God
The Mission of God
The Mission of God
The Mission of God
The Mission of God
The Mission of God
The Mission of God
The Mission of God
The Mission of God
The Mission of God
The Mission of God
The Mission of God
The Mission of God
The Mission of God
The Mission of God
The Mission of God
The Mission of God
The Mission of God
The Mission of God
The Mission of God
The Mission of God
The Mission of God
The Mission of God

The Mission of God
The Mission of God
The Mission of God
The Mission of God
The Mission of God
The Mission of God
The Mission of God
The Mission of God
The Mission of God
The Mission of God
The Mission of God
The Mission of God
The Mission of God
The Mission of God
The Mission of God
The Mission of God
The Mission of God
The Mission of God
The Mission of God
The Mission of God
The Mission of God
The Mission of God
The Mission of God
The Mission of God
The Mission of God
The Mission of God